EGMONT

We bring stories to life

First published in Great Britain in 2006 by Dean,
an imprint of Egmont UK Limited
239 Kensington High Street, London W8 6SA

Thomas the Tank Engine & Friends™

A BRITT ALLCROFT COMPANY PRODUCTION

Based on The Railway Series by The Reverend W Awdry
Photographs © 2006 Gullane (Thomas) LLC. A HIT Entertainment Company

Thomas the Tank Engine & Friends and Thomas & Friends are trademarks of Gullane (Thomas) Limited.
Thomas the Tank Engine & Friends and Design is Reg. US. Pat. & Tm. Off.

ISBN 978 0 6035 6233 4
ISBN 0 6035 6233 7
3 5 7 9 10 8 6 4 2
Printed in Singapore

Edward, the Very Useful Engine

The Thomas TV Series

All the engines on the Island of Sodor were good at different things. Gordon was a very good Express. Percy was good at carrying the mail. And Edward was good at being a back engine.

When engines had heavy loads, Edward would couple up behind them and help push. But Edward was old. Some engines thought that made him unreliable.

"Edward is a useless old steam pot," Gordon sniffed. "He should be retired."

"But he doesn't have tyres," Percy said.

"'Retired' means being taken out of service," explained Thomas.

"And Edward should be retired right now," said Gordon.

The other big engines agreed with him.

When The Fat Controller heard what Gordon had said, he was cross. He went to find Edward.

"Edward, I want you to teach Stepney how to run the new branch line properly," he said.

"But Sir, who will look after the trucks?" asked Edward.

"Duck will do your work," The Fat Controller replied.

When the other engines heard that Duck was going to replace Edward, they were pleased.

"Duck is very reliable," said Henry.

"It makes no difference to me," said Gordon, importantly. "I don't need a back engine."

And he wheeshed away.

Next morning, Duck was busy doing Edward's work. He was not happy. The trucks were playing silly games.

"Duck should play with other ducks,
Cos he's no good at pulling trucks!
Quack! Quack! Quack! Quack!
Hold back! Hold back!" they giggled.

As he chuffed along the line, Duck pulled as hard as he could, but the trucks held him back. He was going slower and slower and slower.

Halfway up Gordon's Hill, his wheels stopped turning. Duck was stuck!

"Oh no," said his Driver. "This is Gordon's line! He'll be coming along any minute now!"

Duck's Driver phoned the Signalman to warn him. But it was too late to switch Gordon on to another line.

"I'll have to put all the signals to red," said the Signalman.

Gordon saw the red signals. He slowed down and stopped just behind Duck.

"You silly engine," said Gordon. "Now I will have to push you up the hill."

Gordon tried to set off again, but his wheels spun and spun. Gordon was stuck too!

"It's no use. We need a back engine," said the Driver.

Gordon was cross! He still thought he didn't need a back engine.

Gordon was even more cross when he saw who was coming to help him. Edward and Stepney had finished their work, so The Fat Controller had sent Edward to be the back engine!

"Hello, Gordon! Hello, Duck!" said Edward happily. "Need some help?"

"Hello, Edward!" said Duck. "Yes, please!"

But Gordon didn't say anything.

Edward buffered up and the strange train set off. At last it chuffed gently into the station.

"Look at that!" laughed a little boy, pointing to Edward. "The back engine must be very strong!"

"He must be a Really Useful Engine," said another passenger.

Gordon was very embarrassed that he needed Edward's help.

Later that day, The Fat Controller spoke crossly to Gordon.

"You have said some very rude things about Edward," The Fat Controller said. "He has proved today that he is helpful and reliable."

Gordon felt ashamed. He rolled up to Edward. "Thank you for helping me," said Gordon. "You really are a Useful Engine."

"It was nothing," said Edward, happily.

Soon, everything was back to normal. Edward was back at his old job, and all the engines were glad of his help – even Gordon!

And there was no more talk of Edward retiring. After all, he was the best back engine on the Island of Sodor!